Kylie Jean

Drama Queen

by Marci Peschke

illustrated by Tuesday Mourning

PICTURE WINDOW BOOKS
a capstone imprint

Kylie Jean is published by Picture Window Books
A Capstone Imprint
1710 Roe Crest Drive
North Mankato, Minnesota 56003
www.capstonepub.com

Library of Congress Cataloging-in-Publication Data
Peschke, M. (Marci).
   Drama queen / by Marci Peschke ; illustrated by Tuesday Mourning.
      p. cm. — (Kylie Jean)
   ISBN 978-1-4048-6757-4 (library binding) — ISBN 978-1-4048-6616-4 (pbk.)
   ISBN 978-1-4048-7617-0 (pbk.)
   [1. Theater—Fiction. 2. Schools—Fiction. 3. Texas—Fiction.] I. Mourning, Tuesday, ill.
II. Title.
   PZ7.P441245Dr 2011
   [Fic]—dc22   2010030656

Summary: Kylie Jean's class is performing Alice in Wonderland! Kylie Jean
knows she'd be just perfect as the Queen of Hearts. But mean girl Paula
wants the part too . . . .

Creative Director: Heather Kindseth
Graphic Designer: Emily Harris
Editor: Beth Brezenoff
Production Specialist: Michelle Biedscheid

Design Element Credit:
Shutterstock/blue67design

Printed in China
082012   006904

For Kristy Marie, with love for Rick
—M.P.

Table of Contents

All About Me, Kylie Jean!

My name is Kylie Jean Carter. I live in a big, sunny, yellow house on Peachtree Lane in Jacksonville, Texas with Momma, Daddy, and my two brothers, T.J. and Ugly Brother.

T.J. is my older brother, and Ugly Brother is . . . well . . . he's really a dog. Don't you go telling him he is a dog. Okay? I mean it. He thinks he is a real true person.

He is a black-and-white bulldog. His front looks like his back, all smashed in. His face is all droopy like he's sad, but he's not.

His two front teeth stick out and his tongue hangs down. (Now you know why his name is Ugly Brother.)

Everyone I love to the moon and back lives in Jacksonville. Nanny, Pa, Granny, Pappy, my aunts, my uncles, and my cousins all live here. I'm extra lucky, because I can see all of them any time I want to!

My momma says I'm pretty. She says I have eyes as blue as the summer sky and a smile as sweet as an angel. (Momma says pretty is as pretty does. That means being nice to the old folks, taking care of little animals, and respecting my momma and daddy.)

But I'm pretty on the outside and on the inside. My hair is long, brown, and curly.

I wear it in a ponytail sometimes, but my absolute most favorite is when Momma pulls it back in a princess style on special days.

I just gave you a little hint about my big dream. Ever since I was a bitty baby I have wanted to be an honest-to-goodness beauty queen. I even know the wave. It's side to side, nice and slow, with a dazzling smile. I practice all the time, because everybody knows beauty queens need to have a perfect wave.

I'm Kylie Jean, and I'm going to be a beauty queen. Just you wait and see!

Chapter One
Summer's Over

On Sunday afternoon, right at the tail end of summer, Momma, Daddy, T.J., and I are all visiting Lickskillet Farm, where Nanny and Pa live. Everybody in my whole family is at the farm for Sunday dinner.

T.J. and the boys are out in the pasture. The grown-ups are talking while they sit in the yard and drink lemonade. The big girls are inside, gossiping.

Everyone is here except Ugly Brother. He had to stay at home.

Me and my best cousin, Lucy, are sitting on the fence. Lucy is exactly the same age as me.

My face is covered up by a big ole slice of sweet pink watermelon. Pink is my most favorite color.

Lucy looks at me and laughs.

"What's so funny?" I ask.

"You've been eating that melon right straight down the middle. It looks like a heart," she says. "Plus, there's pink juice drippin' off your chin."

"Watermelon only tastes good when it's messy," I say. Then I whisper, "I just love spittin' the seeds out, too. Don't you tell anyone. That is not how beauty queens act."

I spit out three little black seeds. They fly like little black bugs and land one by one in the pasture. Plop, plop, plop.

Lucy crosses her heart. "I promise to never ever tell that Kylie Jean Carter is a seed-spitter," she says.

We both spit out more seeds. They shoot into the pasture and land in little black piles.

Our dusty legs swing over the rail as we sit and spit. I smile up at the hot sun as it kisses all of my little brown freckles.

It is a good day for the last day of summer.

Tomorrow is the first day of school, but we have the rest of the afternoon to play at the farm.

After Lucy and I finish our watermelon, we run through the tall gold grass into the mud next to the pond. I can feel it squishing between my toes. Then we slip our dirty bare feet into the warm blue water. The pond smells good, like rain.

When it is almost dark, the mosquitoes start to bite, and Lucy keeps slapping her legs.

"We better go on in," Lucy says. "It's time for supper."

We walk toward the tiny white farmhouse right in the middle of a hot pink watermelon sky. Black birds fly by like little black seeds.

Summer is almost gone, and the sun is going away, too. It is a shimmering orange ball floating lazily near the ground. Lightning bugs start to flicker in the grass. Today is almost over.

Tomorrow will be a big adventure. My heart starts to pound. Tomorrow, I will be in a whole new grade at Lee Elementary School.

Chapter Two

A New Teacher

I don't sleep one little itty-bitty teeny tiny wink
that night. No sir. Going to second grade is too
exciting!

On Monday morning, I sit up in my bed
and look around my room. I see my new pink

backpack with hearts
on it. Then I see my new
pink sneakers with silver
laces. After that, I see my
pile of school supplies.

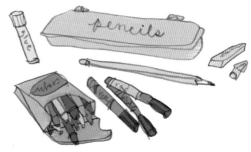

My pink pencil box is full of pencils, a glue stick,
erasers, crayons, and markers. I am ready!

I hop out of bed and get dressed. I picked out my outfit last night, so it is all ready for me.

I put on my blue skirt with the ruffles, my new pink top, and my tiara.

"T.J. and Kylie Jean," Momma calls, "come and get your breakfast. You're going to be late on your first day if you don't hurry up!"

I rush downstairs to the big sunny kitchen. Momma made pancakes and bacon for us to eat. T.J.'s pancakes are normal, but Momma made mine so they look like hearts.

T.J. is already eating when I sit down. "You better hurry up," he says with his mouth full. "You know Mr. Jim won't wait for us if you're late."

Mr. Jim is the man who drives our school bus. Some kids think he's mean, but I like him.

Ugly Brother comes to the table too. He sits down next to me and looks at me with his big brown eyes.

"You just have to eat some of this tasty bacon," I tell him. Under the table, I feed him three pieces of bacon. Ugly Brother gobbles them up. Then he licks my fingers real good.

"Do you like bacon?" I ask him.

"Ruff, ruff," he replies.

Two barks mean yes. One bark means no. He likes it!

"Come on, Kylie Jean," T.J. says. "Quit feedin' the dog. We have to go."

I run to the kitchen sink and wash my hands good. Then I'm ready to go!

My backpack is loaded up with school supplies. When I swing it on to my back I nearly topple right over.

My big brother is getting awful bossy now. He just grabs my hand and drags me to the front door. In his other hand, he is holding my new lunch box with red hearts on the front. "Come on, now," he tells me.

"Bye, Ugly Brother. Bye, Momma. Love you, " I shout. T.J. slams the door behind us.

The big yellow bus full of new faces pulls up right in front of our house. Mr. Jim opens the bus door. T.J. has to push me up the steps because my backpack is so heavy.

Mr. Jim waves us to the back of the bus. It's hot and smells like Cheetos in here.

The bus is crowded, so T.J. and I have to squeeze in a seat with one of his friends.

First, the bus pulls up in front of the high school. "See ya later, Lil' Bit," T.J. tells me. When he and his friend are gone, I have more room. I scoot over to the window and watch T.J. walk into the high school. Then Mr. Jim drives away.

Before long, Mr. Jim parks the bus in front of Robert E. Lee Elementary School. The bus door opens and kids roll out like shiny new marbles. I get pushed along with the crowd, out of the bus, up the sidewalk, and into the building.

Inside the school, all the kids are looking for their new classrooms. Momma told me just where to go. I head straight to Room 101.

My new teacher is standing in the doorway. She is very beautiful. Her hair is brown, darker than mine, and her dress is bright blue with big hot pink flowers on it. I like her already! All teachers should wear something pink.

"Hello," she says, smiling at me. "I like your tiara! Go on in, choose a desk, and find the cubby with your name on it."

"All right," I tell her, smiling back.

Inside Room 101, the desks are pushed together to make little squares. Each square is made up of four desks.

There is a row of cubbies against one of the sky-blue walls. I find my name on one of them and put my backpack in my new cubby.

"Hey, Kylie Jean!" someone says. I look and see my friend Cara sitting nearby. I sit right down next to her.

"Is Lucy here yet?" I ask. Cara shakes her head. I gasp. "Late to school on the first day?" I whisper. That's not like Lucy!

Then an idea hits my brain like mud on a noonday pig. I'm going to save Lucy a desk! The one right across from me will do just fine.

But before I can put my new pink pencil box on that desk, a tall new girl sits down right in the spot I want for Lucy.

"I'm new," she says. "My name is Paula. But you may call me Miss Paula Dupree." Then she holds her hand out to shake mine.

I do not like her already! She just walked right over and stole Lucy's spot!

I don't shake her hand. "Then you may call me Your Majesty," I say, pointing at my tiara. I add, "And you may be Miss Paula Dupree, but you're sittin' in my cousin Lucy's spot. Please move!"

Paula glares at me. She looks down at the desk and then back up. "I don't see her name on it, so it's mine now," she says.

"You could move over one seat," Cara says.

"No, I could not," Paula tells her. "The teacher said to choose a desk, and I chose this one. This is a free country and we don't have a queen," she adds, looking right at my tiara. "And besides, I was here first."

"Please?" I ask nicely.

Paula shakes her head. "No way," she says. She crosses her arms and rolls her eyes at me.

I'm too mad to say anything. I just walk over and put my pink pencil box on the desk across from Cara. I guess my best cousin won't get to sit across from me.

"I'll trade with you, Kylie Jean," Cara offers. "Then you can sit across from Lucy."

"Oh, thank you!" I say. "That is so kind!" I narrow my eyes at Paula. She looks away.

Finally, Lucy runs into the room. I wave at her and point at my pink pencil box.

"Sit here!" I say.

Lucy puts her backpack in the cubby with her name on it. Then she sits down across from me and looks at Paula. "Are you new?" Lucy asks Paula.

"I am indeed. You may call me Miss Paula Dupree," Paula says. Then she sticks her nose up in the air. She is really bugging me, this new girl! I don't think I like her!

Lucy laughs. "I think I'll call you Paula," she says. "What you said is too long, and I'm sure I'll forget it." She winks at me. My cousin can tell from looking at me that I'm mad enough to spit nails!

Just then, the bell rings, and our teacher closes the door. She walks up to the board. Her pretty dress swishes as she walks. On the board, she writes, "My name is Ms. Corazón."

Our new teacher looks at the students in Room 101.

"Good morning, students!" she says. "Welcome to second grade. I have planned so many fun things for us to do this year. We will take trips, do experiments, and even put on a class play. I just know you'll love second grade!"

We all smile at her, even Paula.
"First I will take attendance,"
Ms. Corazón says, "and
then we will start with
today's lessons."

She picks up a piece of
paper and starts calling out
names.

The names are in ABC order.
Alice, Cara, Danny, Eva,
Greg, Hanna, Jessie, Kylie.

When she calls my name, I say, "Here!" and
raise my hand.

Ms. Corazón sees my raised hand and frowns.
She asks, "Kylie, is something wrong?"

I nod. "My real name is Kylie Jean," I say. "I have two parts to my name."

Ms. Corazón smiles. She picks up a pencil and writes on her paper. "Okay, Kylie Jean," she says. "I made a note on my attendance sheet. I won't forget the second part of your name again!"

She continues calling names. Lucy, Mark, Nico, Paula. Paula raises her hand and waves it in the air like a chicken flapping its wings.

"Yes, Paula?" Ms. Corazón asks.

Paula stands up. "My name is Miss Paula Dupree," she says loudly. "Please change it on your paper."

Ms. Corazón raises her eyebrows. Then she frowns. "Paula, you're still a young lady," she says. "I'll just call you Paula."

This makes Paula mad! She crosses her arms and her eyes look as dark as thunder clouds. She looks over at me and sticks out her tongue.

Beauty queens do not stick out their tongues. Ignoring her is the best plan. I just keep my eyes on Ms. Corazón. I can tell already she's going to be the best teacher ever!

Chapter Three
Class Play

All morning, we work on reading. Then we go to art class. My friends and I ignore Paula as best as we can, but it's awful hard. The first thing she does in art class is complain about the aprons we have to wear. She says they smell bad. Well, they do, but she doesn't have to be a baby about it!

When we get back to Room 101, Ms. Corazón waits until we're all sitting down. Then she says, "It's time for lunch, but first, I have something very exciting to tell you."

We all wait.

Ms. Corazón goes on, "We'll be doing *Alice in Wonderland* for our class play! I know y'all will love it."

A lot of kids raise their hands to ask questions, but Ms. Corazón shakes her head. "Time for lunch," she says. "We can talk more about the play later. Please line up at the door."

My friends and I sit together in the cafeteria. We all brought our lunches from home. Paula gets in line for hot lunch. Then she stands in the front of the cafeteria, looking for a place to sit.

It must be real hard to be the new girl.

I get up and run over to her. "Come on, Paula," I say. "You can sit with us." She doesn't look sure, but she follows me back to our table anyway.

Just like Momma says, pretty is as pretty does. I know I have to try to be nice to Paula, even if she's mean.

Paula puts her tray on the table right next to my lunchbox. Then she plops down in her chair. She looks at my lunchbox.

"I don't bring my lunch," she tells us. "My parents aren't poor, so I can buy my lunch at school."

It takes all my strength to hold my tongue!

I take my sandwich, chips, apple slices, and chocolate chip cookies out of my red heart lunchbox.

There's a folded-up piece of paper in the bottom. I open it up.

Kylie Jean,

Have a great
first day at
school.

Love,
Momma

X O X O X O

Paula grabs my note. She reads it, laughs, and wads it up into a ball. "You must be a big baby if your mom has to put notes in your lunch to keep you from crying at school," she says. "Do you miss your mama, Kylie Jean? Boo hoo, you big baby!"

Now I'm really mad. I open my mouth to say something, but Cara does first.

"Paula, Kylie Jean isn't a baby. Her mom just does that to be nice. And we can buy our lunch, but we don't because school lunch tastes super gross," Cara says.

"That's true," I say. I look at Paula's lunch. It looks pretty gross. The lettuce is brown and the pepperoni pizza is all mushy. I would never want to eat it!

I repeat to myself, *Pretty is as pretty does.*

Then I look at Paula. "I know you made fun of my lunch," I say, "but I'll give you half of my turkey sandwich. Do you want it?"

Paula looks at the greasy pizza and brown salad on her tray. Then she shrugs and reaches for half of my sandwich. She eats it in two bites.

"I think *Alice in Wonderland* is perfect for our class play. Don't you?" I ask my friends.

Lucy laughs. "You just want to be the Queen of Hearts," she says.

"Yep!" I say. I sure do want to be the Queen. "If I am, I'll get to wear a real crown," I add, pointing to the sparkly tiara on my head.

Paula rolls her eyes. "Your tiara is dumb," she says. "And it's not real."

"Hush your mouth, Paula," Cara tells her. "Quit pickin' on Kylie Jean."

Paula gets up. "I don't want to sit with a bunch of babies," she tells us.

She picks up her tray and storms away.

My friends and I look at each other. "I'm glad she's gone," I whisper.

"She's mean," Lucy says.

I nod.

"We're not babies," Cara says.

I nod.

But I can tell from my friends' faces that they feel just as bad as I do.

Chapter Four
Getting Ready
for Wonderland

After recess, I stop to get a drink of water. When I'm done, Paula is standing in the doorway of Room 101. She steps in front of me when I try to walk through the door.

I move to the right, but she moves too! Then I move to the left, and she steps right in front of me again!

Finally, I push past her.

Lucy and Cara are waiting at our desks. "Did she try to keep you out?" Cara asks. "We should start calling her Paula DuMEAN!"

I frown. I don't know for sure if Cara is right. Name-calling is mean, too, and beauty queens aren't mean.

"Momma always says you have to act pretty to be pretty," I say quietly.

I look over at Paula. She's still standing in the doorway. Now she's trying to block Hanna from coming into our room. Hanna is real little, and she looks like she might cry.

Room 101

"Paula's mean," Cara tells me. "If she's mean, we can be mean back."

Ms. Corazón walks up to the door. "Please find your seat, girls," she says to Paula and Hanna, smiling.

Paula quickly runs to her desk and sits down. Hanna slowly walks to her seat.

"Let's get started with *Alice in Wonderland*!" Ms. Corazón says.

She's carrying a stack of booklets. She walks around the room, handing one booklet to each student.

"On Friday, we'll have tryouts for all of the parts," Ms. Corazón tells us. "There are sixteen parts in the play."

I look around the room. There are more than sixteen kids in my class. But Ms. Corazón sees my worried look and adds, "Some people won't be in the play. That's okay, because we need some kids to help move things around on the stage. They're called stagehands, and they work behind the scenes."

Being a stagehand is not for me. I'm only going to practice the part of the Queen of Hearts.

Right from the very beginning, I knew it was the part for me! She's not a beauty queen, but she gets to wear a crown.

I open the booklet to page one. I need to get down to business. By Friday, I want to know all of the words without looking at the paper.

Chapter 5
After School

The day seems to drag on for hours. When the three o'clock bell finally rings, I run out of Room 101. I don't stop running until I get out to the bus and hop on. I'm the very first person on the bus!

"What's your hurry?" Mr. Jim asks. "Bad day at school?"

I shake my head. "No sir," I tell him. "I just need to get home real quick."

Mr. Jim smiles. "Well, it might be a minute," he says. "You have to wait for all the other kids, and then we have to pick up the high school kids."

I sigh. This might take longer than I thought! "All right," I say. I down sit in the first seat in the front row. That way I can get off the bus faster. Then I have to wait and wait some more. Soon all of the kids from Lee Elementary are on the bus. Mr. Jim nods at me. Then we take off for the high school.

T.J. is the last high school kid on the bus. "Hey, Lil' Bit," he says, sitting down next to me.

I'm mad at him for taking so long, so I decide not to talk to him all the way home! I just turn away and stare out the window.

"What did I do?" T.J. asks. When I don't answer, he just sighs. "Whatever, Kylie Jean," he grumbles.

When we get to our house on Peachtree Lane, I fly off the bus and zoom straight for the front door. T.J. walks slower and comes in after me.

I holler, "Ugly Brother!" and run through the living room to the kitchen.

Momma is in the kitchen, making us an afternoon snack. I sit down at the table and call for Ugly Brother again.

"Ugly Brother is at the vet with your daddy," Momma says. "Remember? He's getting his shots today."

That makes me feel terrible! My poor Ugly Brother. I put my head in my hands.

Momma smiles a nice smile. She can tell I feel
bad.

She slides a plate of
warm brownies in front
of me. She used a cookie
cutter to make them into
hearts!

"Why don't you tell me all about your first day
at school, sugar?" Momma asks. "Was it good?"

I shrug and stuff a brownie in my mouth. "Parf
of if wath goob," I tell her. Then I swallow and try
again. "Part of it was good," I say. "But part of it
was bad."

"What was bad?" Momma asks.

"There's a new girl," I tell her. I fill her in on
Paula.

Momma frowns. "I don't like the idea of someone calling you a baby," she says. "But I think you made too big of a deal about the desk for Lucy. Paula didn't steal Lucy's seat. Ms. Corazón said you could all choose your seats. And Lucy was the one who was late to school!"

I nod. "I know, Momma," I say. "But then I tried to be nice, and Paula was real mean."

Momma shakes her head. "Pretty is as pretty does," she says. "What else happened today? What was the good part?"

I start telling Momma what stagehands are, but she already knows. So we talk about the play. I tell her about all the different parts.

"Let me guess," Momma says. "You want to be Alice."

"No way, Momma!" I say. "First of all, Alice has 125 lines, so Ms. Corazón says four girls have to play Alice. I want to be the only one playing my part."

"What part is that?" Momma asks.

"The Queen of Hearts!" I say. "Of course."

"And how many lines does the Queen of Hearts have?" Momma asks, reaching over to straighten my tiara.

"Thirty-two," I tell her. "I already memorized two. That means I only have thirty left to go, and then I'll know them all! But how can I learn all the lines?"

"Copy them down over and over again," Momma says. "When I was in plays in college, that always helped me."

"Momma!" I whisper, shocked. "I never knew you were a famous actress!"

Momma laughs. "I wasn't famous, Kylie Jean," she says. Then she winks and adds, "There's a lot you don't know about your momma! Now finish your snack and run upstairs to practice."

I finish up the crumbs of brownies and head upstairs. I find a pretty pencil with a heart-shaped eraser and a pad of paper with pink hearts on it. They will help me get in the mood to be the Queen.

I start copying the Queen of Hearts's lines from the play book Ms. Corazón passed out. But after I write about ten lines down, my hand starts to hurt. Then I hear the front door close.

"Ugly Brother!" I shout.

I run downstairs. My poor dog is standing there, with his tail down. He's walking slow and looks real sad.

I bend down next to him. "Did it hurt?" I whisper, putting my arms around him.

"Ruff, ruff," he barks quietly. That means yes. Poor Ugly Brother.

I stand up. "I have just the thing to make you feel better," I tell him. "Come on!"

When Ugly Brother sees that I'm walking into the kitchen, his ears perk up and he slowly follows me.

First I find the stepstool. Then I take down two bowls from the cupboard and find some vanilla ice cream in the freezer.

Momma walks in as I'm scooping ice cream into the bowls. "What are you doing, Kylie Jean?" she asks.

"Making Ugly Brother feel better," I tell her.

"Who's the other bowl for?" Momma asks.

"Me, of course!" I say.

"Oh, Kylie Jean," Momma says. She smiles. "Sometimes I don't know what to do with you."

Chapter Six
Tryouts

After school on Tuesday, I know I need to get down to business. I only have three days left till the tryouts, and I only have five lines memorized.

First things first, I need to look like the Queen of Hearts. In my closet, I find the Little Red Riding Hood cape I wore for Halloween last year.

I put it on and look in the mirror. Close, but not close enough.

I find some white socks and pins in Momma's room. I pin the socks around the edge of my cape, so it looks like a fur trim.

Next, I cut out a giant red heart from some paper in my room. I glue glitter all over it. You can't be a queen without some sparkle! I pin the heart to the back of my cape. Then I add a gold crown.

I look in the mirror. I think I look great, but I need a second opinion. "Ugly Brother!" I yell. He comes running into the room. "How do I look?" I ask. "Do I look right for the part?"

He barks, "Ruff, ruff!"

Two barks! That means yes!

I decide I'll wear the outfit all week whenever I'm at home. That way, by Friday, I'll be ready. Momma says this is called getting into character.

In the morning, I practice while we eat.

Momma sets the breakfast table with a pretty teapot so I can practice pouring the tea.

"More tea?" I ask the White Rabbit.

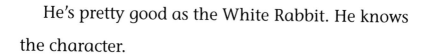

Ugly Brother says, "Ruff, ruff!"

He's pretty good as the White Rabbit. He knows the character.

After school, we practice in the back yard.

"Off with their heads!" I yell.

That part scares Ugly Brother, so he puts his paws over his eyes.

At bedtime, we practice too. I shout, "Bring me the Duchess!"

Ugly Brother brings me a Barbie. For practice, Barbie makes an okay Duchess.

By Friday morning, I'm ready. That's good, because T.J. is really sick of me practicing. "Off with your head, Kylie Jean!" he says when I come down to breakfast. "I'm so sick of the Queen of Hearts! I can even hear you in my sleep."

"Stop it, T.J.," Momma says. "How did you sleep, Kylie Jean? Are you ready for your big day?"

"Yes ma'am," I tell her. "I sure am!"

"Where's your costume?" Daddy asks.

"I don't need it today," I announce. I shake my hair. I'm wearing my sparkly red heart barrettes. "These barrettes will show that I am the true Queen of Hearts," I explain.

Daddy stands up. "I better get to work," he says. "Break a leg, honey."

I frown. "Daddy, are you being mean to me?" I ask quietly.

Daddy smiles. "That's show-biz talk," he explains. "It means good luck."

"Oh!" I say. "Thanks, Daddy."

I start to get nervous on the bus. "Calm down, Lil' Bit," T.J. says before he gets off at the high school. "You'll be great. I bet nobody practiced near as much as you did."

When the bus stops at Lee Elementary School, I go straight to Room 101. Ms. Corazón is at the door waiting to greet us. She says, "Good morning, Kylie Jean! I like your barrettes."

Cara and Lucy are waiting for me at our desks. I smile and wave, nice and slow, side to side, like a true beauty queen. "Good morning!" I say.

Then I hear a loud voice coming from the classroom door. I turn around and my mouth falls right open.

Paula Dupree is standing in the door. She's wearing a Queen of Hearts costume. She looks just like the queen in the movie, and I know, because I watched it ten times this week.

Cara whispers, "Do you two see Paula DuMean?"

Lucy nods. Then she says, "Don't worry, Kylie Jean. You'll be so good, no one will notice her fancy costume. You have on your pretty red heart barrettes."

Tears come to my eyes. I worked so hard, and now I don't have the right clothes to be Queen.

Lucy whispers, "Queens don't cry in front of people, Kylie Jean."

I nod. She's right. Queens aren't babies. I take a deep breath and smile.

Later, we all read our parts for Ms. Corazón. I'm the only person who doesn't have to read from the play book, because I know all my lines by heart.

I make my voice loud when the Queen is mad and quiet when she is thinking.

Just like I thought, Paula wants to be the Queen of Hearts, too. But she has to read all her lines.

When she's done, I say, "You did a good job."

I think Paula will tell me I did a good job, too, but she just says, "I know."

Ms. Corazón says, "It's going to be very hard to choose just one of you to be the Queen of Hearts."

I smile at her and turn my head so she'll notice my heart barrettes. Ms. Corazón winks at me. Then she says, "Everyone who tried out will get a part. I'll tell you all on Monday!"

I can hardly wait. I just know she's going to pick me!

Chapter Seven
Cast Assignments

Luckily, the weekend goes real fast, and before I know it, it's Monday morning!

Today, T.J. doesn't have to bug me. I get ready and eat my breakfast lickety-split. I run out the door and am waiting for the bus ten minutes before it's supposed to get there.

When I finally get to school, a bunch of kids are standing in front of Room 101. I am too short to see, so I keep jumping up and down trying to see over them.

Cara is close to the front, reading the paper on the door. She pushes her way out. Then she sees me.

"Did I get the part of the Queen?" I ask.

"Well, you did get a part," Cara replies, looking down at the ground.

"The Queen?" I ask again.

She shakes her head. "Alice!" she tells me.

That can't be right. I don't even have yellow hair like Alice does! Maybe it's a mistake. It's just a bad dream. Maybe I'm asleep and still dreaming.

"Cara, pinch me, quick!" I beg.

Cara reaches over and pinches me. Hard. Too hard!

"OUCH!" I shout.

"Sorry," Cara says. "Come on, let's go sit down."

I follow her to our desks. Paula is already sitting down. She says, "Congratulations, Alice. You know, you have the star role, but I get to play the Queen. It's the perfect part for me. I love giving orders."

I can't believe my ears. Paula DuMean gets to be the Queen! How could Ms. Corazón give her the part? Paula didn't even know all her lines. I did. Why can't I be the Queen?

As soon as Ms. Corazón walks in, I run over to her quick as I can. "How are you today, Kylie Jean?" she asks, smiling at me as she puts a stack of papers on her desk.

"Well, to be honest, ma'am, I'm not so good," I tell her.

Ms. Corazón frowns. "What's the matter?" she asks.

I sigh. "I think you must have made a mistake when you did the parts for the play," I explain. "I'm the one who's supposed to be the Queen. Paula didn't even know her lines! And did you forget that I have brown hair? Alice has yellow hair."

"I know you have brown hair," Ms. Corazón says. She grins at me. "I have a surprise for you!" She reaches into one of her desk drawers and pulls out a big, floppy blond wig.

"You'll get to wear this during the play," Ms. Corazón says.

"But I still think I should be the Queen of Hearts," I tell her. I don't want to touch the wig. It looks weird. She lets it fall onto her desk.

"Kylie Jean, I gave the role of Alice to the girls who did the best job memorizing their lines," Ms. Corazón tells me. She smiles. "And you were the very best at memorizing!"

"But I didn't want to be Alice," I tell her. I feel tears stinging my eyes like little bees. "I wanted to be the Queen."

Ms. Corazón nods. She pats my hand. "I understand," she says. "But Paula is going to be the Queen."

She looks at me for a moment. Then she adds, "I'll tell you what. If Paula gets sick, or can't be the Queen, you can be her understudy."

When she sees my confused look, she explains, "That's the person who steps in if an actor can't perform."

"Okay," I say sadly. "I guess that's better than nothin'." But I know it's not. I'm doomed to play Alice while Paula DuMean gets the role of the Queen of Hearts.

For the rest of the day, I feel worse than a dog on a short leash.

Chapter Eight
Being Alice

When I get home from school, I'm still feeling lower than a doodle bug. I don't want to eat the peanut butter and apple snack Momma makes for me. I don't want to play with Ugly Brother. I don't want to do anything.

But I know I have to put a smile on my face and try. I can't just up and quit, so I have to learn Alice's lines.

Ugly Brother walks over and sits down next to the kitchen table. He rests his head on my feet because he can tell I'm sad.

"You did a good job of helping me with being the Queen," I tell Ugly Brother. He looks up at me with his big brown eyes. I reach down and pat him. "But we have to start over after all our hard work," I say. "I'm going to be Alice. Will you please help me again?"

He replies, "Ruff, ruff!"

I pull the yellow wig from my backpack and put it on. Ugly Brother goes crazy barking. Then he runs out of the kitchen and into the living room. He hides behind the couch.

"Silly!" I shout, getting up to follow him. "It's me, Kylie Jean! Your sister!" I peek over the back of the couch.

"Ruff!" Ugly Brother barks.

Momma walks in to see what all the hollering is about. "Maybe you should practice without the wig," she suggests.

I take it off. Then Ugly Brother comes over and jumps up on me like I've been gone away on vacation or something. He licks my face. "Let's get to work," I tell him.

Alice talks to everyone, so now Ugly Brother has to be lots of different people. Sometimes he gets confused and doesn't know who he's supposed to be. I'm Alice Number 1, so all of my lines are in the beginning of the play.

Some kids didn't get parts with lines. They'll be mushrooms or flowers. I know I'm lucky, but I still wish I could be the Queen.

Chapter Nine
Practice Makes Perfect

Lucy, Cara, Sophie, and I are the four Alices. Sophie has to wear the wig too. Her real hair is red. All the Alices have to share a costume. That's okay, except Cara is tall. When she wears the costume the skirt is kind of short.

On Tuesday, we practice the play after lunch. I'm trying to be the best Alice I can.

I'm glad that I don't have to be Alice when Paula is playing the Queen of Hearts. That would make me too sad. But Cara is the Alice in that scene.

My part is fun. I get to play Alice when she is getting big and small. When she's big, I stand on a box. When she's small, I crouch down.

After practice, Ms. Corazón tells me I'm doing a wonderful job. "Who helps you practice?" she asks. "Your mother?"

"Nope," I tell her. "Ugly Brother helps me most of the time."

Ms. Corazón frowns. "You shouldn't call your brother names," she says. "What's his real name?"

"His name is Bruno," I say. "But everybody calls him Ugly Brother. Even Momma!"

Ms. Corazón shakes her head. "That poor boy," she says sadly.

"He's fine, ma'am," I say. "He did have shots last week, but he's okay now. I've been giving him doggy treats and ice cream whenever he helps me!"

Now she looks shocked. I head back over to my desk and sit down. "I don't know why Ms. Corazón is so worried about my dog!" I whisper to Lucy.

Lucy shrugs. "Maybe you've been giving him too much ice cream," she says.

Chapter 10
Red Spots

On Wednesday morning, we start to paint the set for our play. The set is the decorations that will go up behind us so the audience knows where we are.

When I walk into Room 101 in the morning, there are long pieces of paper laid out on the floor. There are designs drawn on each paper, like they're pages from a huge coloring book. I see mushrooms, flowers, trees, grass, and a sky with fluffy clouds.

Lucy, Cara, and I get busy painting.

I start with a big mushroom. Ms. Corazón tells me to make it red and white. She tells Lucy to make her cloud white and make the sky blue. Cara's flower should be pink, with a green stem.

Soon, I have paint on my jeans. I look around and see that lots of kids have paint all over them. I'm glad I didn't wear a fancy dress to school today.

As I'm looking around the room, Paula catches my eye. She stands up, puts her paintbrush down, and starts walking toward me.

I whisper, "Oh no, here comes Paula!"

Paula stands over us and looks down at our pieces of the set. She says, "I see you girls need help. You aren't very creative. I like to do my own designs, and I finished more pieces than anybody."

She points at a few papers on the other side of the room. I can see that she didn't take her time. She made the mushrooms blue. She made the sky green. She made the trees pink.

Normally, I would love pink trees. After all, pink is my color. But that's not how it's supposed to look!

Lucy and I look at each other. I know what she's thinking. We don't need help from someone who thinks the sky is green!

"We're going to follow Ms. Corazón's directions, but thanks anyway," Lucy replies.

Paula frowns. "Suit yourself, if you want ugly, baby drawings," she says.

"It's not babyish to follow directions," Cara says.

"Well, it's babyish to get paint all over yourself," Paula says, pointing at Cara's shirt. There's a splash of green paint on her blue shirt. "I'm the Queen," Paula goes on, looking at me. "And Queens don't get paint on themselves."

I look down at the splatters of paint on my jeans.

Paula stomps away. "Just ignore her," I tell my friends. "She doesn't know the first thing about being a Queen."

We paint all morning. After lunch, we have recess. "Let's play color tag!" Cara shouts.

If you haven't played color tag before, you sure are missing out on the most fun game. One person shouts a color. If you have on that color, nobody can tag you. Since we're all covered in paint, we have on lots of colors.

Paula gets tagged a lot, since she's only wearing blue jeans, red sneakers, and a green shirt. She has no paint colors on her. By the time the game is over, I'm hot from running around so much.

After math we're going to paint some more, so we can be all finished by tomorrow for our final dress rehearsal. That means we will practice the play just like we're really doing it.

We will have our performance on Friday. Momma and Daddy are both going to come. Daddy even took the day off from work!

During math, I see that Paula has a red spot on her forehead. I talk right in Lucy's ear.

I whisper, "Paula has a zit on her forehead just like T.J. gets."

Lucy whispers back, "It's probably paint."

"Nuh-uh. She didn't get any paint on her, remember?" I say.

"What is it, then?" Lucy asks.

I shrug.

By the time painting starts again, I notice three more spots on Paula's face. Plus, she's all sweaty. She keeps scratching her arms and her tummy.

"What's wrong with you?" I whisper.

"Shut up, you big baby," Paula says back. "Leave me alone."

I can't believe she called me a name AND told me to shut up! Rude! But I don't want to tell on her. I think she might be getting sick or something.

I walk over to Ms. Corazón, who is helping Taylor with his White Rabbit costume. She smiles when she sees me. "What's up, Kylie Jean?" she asks.

"I'm getting awful worried about Paula, ma'am," I tell her. "She has spots on her, and it's not paint either."

Ms. Corazón puts down her sewing needle lickety split. She dashes over to Paula.

"Let me look at your face, honey," Ms. Corazón says. Paula sticks her tongue out at me. She knows I'm the one who told Ms. Corazón about her spots.

"I think I better get you down to the nurse," Ms. Corazón tells Paula.

We keep on painting while they're gone, but I keep glancing at the door. I'm worried about Paula.

Even though she's the meanest girl I have ever met in my whole entire life.

When Ms. Corazón comes back, she claps her hands.

"Everyone, please listen up," she says. We all quiet down. "Paula has the chicken pox," she tells us.

Lucy nods. "I had that one time," she says. "I hated it! My mom made me wear socks on my hands so I wouldn't scratch!"

"I'm going to write a note for each of you to bring home," Ms. Corazón tells us.

I raise my hand. "What about the play?" I ask. "Will Paula be better in time for Friday?"

Ms. Corazón sighs. "I don't think so," she says. "I think you'll have to do her part, Kylie Jean, since you're her understudy."

I want to shout and scream with joy, but I don't. Inside, I feel my heart pounding, like I'm scared, but really I'm super happy. I don't want Paula to be sick, but I sure am glad to be Queen!

Chapter Eleven
Not So Mean

When I get home, I tell Momma all about Paula getting the chicken pox. Momma is glad that I'm going to be the Queen. But I can't stop thinking about Paula. Nobody likes her. She won't even get one visitor. Momma always visits sick friends and takes them a pot of soup.

"Ugly Brother, do you think I should visit Paula?" I ask.

He whines and covers his face with his paws. That means he thinks it's a bad idea, but I already made up my mind. Paula needs a friend.

I'm too little to make soup, so I pack some cookies and apple juice in my backpack. Then I pack my favorite book, *Ramona the Pest*, too.

Momma is on the phone, so I don't bother to ask her if I can go. I know she'd want me to do nice things for Paula.

"I'm going to a friend's house, but I'll be back for dinner," I shout. I hop on my pink bike with the sparkly streamers and ride to Paula's house. She lives on the same street as Cara.

When I get there, I ring the bell. *Ding-dong.*

Finally, the door opens. It's a lady. I guess it must be Paula's mom. She has a big belly. Not like she ate too many cookies, but like she's going to have a baby.

"Can I help you, honey?" she asks.

"I'm here to see Paula," I tell her. "I'm Kylie Jean. A friend. From school."

The lady smiles. "Oh!" she says. "How nice! But Paula's sick, honey. You don't want to get the chicken pox!"

"Oh," I say. "Well, what if I just go in her room?" I ask. "I won't touch her or anything. I just want to say hi."

Paula's mom thinks for a second.

Finally, she smiles. "I guess that'd be all right," she says. "But only for a second."

"Promise," I say. I cross my heart to show her I mean it.

Paula's mom leads me to Paula's room. "Paula?" she says. "Someone's here to see you." She smiles at me and says, "I'll be back in a minute." Then she walks away.

Paula is lying in her bed, watching TV. Her face is covered with spots. She asks, "What are you doing here, Kylie Jean?"

"I brought you some cookies," I tell her. Then I reach into my backpack and pull out the bag of cookies. She eyes the bag, and I can tell she wants a cookie. I pop one in my mouth. "You want one?" I ask.

Paula nods.

"Okay, but I promised not to touch you, so we'll have to be real quick," I say.

I hold out the cookie. "Grab the other end," I tell her.

Paula reaches for the cookie. Our fingers don't touch when she takes it.

She gobbles up the cookie faster than Ugly Brother can chew up a doggie treat.

I look around.

Her room is painted blue. There's a big easel for coloring, like a real artist would have. Paula has painted a pink mushroom on it. Her Queen of Hearts costume is hanging up on the closet door.

"I like your room," I tell her.

Paula frowns. "Pretty soon I will have to share with the new baby."

"Is your momma having a baby?" I ask.

"Yep," Paula tells me. "It's gonna be a girl." She sighs. "I really wanted a brother. Oh well."

"I have a brother," I tell her. "It's not that great."

"Why'd you come over?" Paula asks.

I shrug. "I don't know," I say. "I thought you'd be lonely. I brought you a book and some juice."

Paula frowns again. "Who's gonna be my part in the play?"

"I am," I tell her.

She looks away for a minute.

Then she says, "Well, I guess you'll be needin' a costume." She points at the Queen of Hearts outfit hanging on the closet door. "You can try on mine."

"Okay," I say. I pull the dress over my head and put on her crown. The dress makes a red puddle at my feet. It is too long, but the cape and the crown both fit. "I bet my momma could sew this to make it shorter," I say. "If it would be okay with you."

For the first time ever, Paula smiles.

"I really wanted to hate you, but I can't," she says. "It was real nice of you to come over to my house. That is the nicest thing that's happened to me since I moved here. So I guess you can make my costume shorter," she tells me. "But you better take it off now. I think my mom will come back soon."

I take off the costume and stuff it into my backpack. Just then, Paula's mom walks back in. "It's time to go, Kylie Jean," she says. "Thanks for coming by."

"Feel better, Paula," I say. "I hope you come back to school soon."

"Thanks for coming over," Paula says. She smiles at me and I wink at her.

As I ride my bike home, I think, *You never can have too many friends.*

Chapter Twelve
Actress Divine

It only takes Momma a minute to sew up the dress so that it fits me. She can sew fast as lightning! I have a pair of shoes that match perfectly. I twirl in front of the mirror in her room.

"You look nice, Kylie Jean," Momma tells me. "I can't wait to see you in the play!"

The next day, I decide I want to wear the costume to school. I put on my gown, shoes, and the cape. I look just like the Queen!

After lunch, when it's time to practice the play, I have to change into my Alice costume. I have to play Alice first. Later I will be the Queen of Hearts.

During the dress rehearsal, even though I'm playing two parts, I don't make one little teeny tiny mistake.

Mr. Peterson, our principal, comes in to watch us. When the play is over, he shakes each of our hands and tells us we did a good job. He shakes my hand and says, "You were a wonderful Queen!"

"She was Alice, too," Cara tells him.

"Wow!" Mr. Peterson says. "That's a lot of lines!"

After school, I get on the bus.

"Mr. Jim, you just have to come see me in the play tomorrow. If you do, I will be happy as a bee in honey!" I exclaim.

Mr. Jim has heard all my lines. I just know he won't want to miss the play.

He nods and smiles when I invite him. "Sure thing, Miss Kylie Jean," he says. "I'll be there tomorrow. I reckon I should see it since a bunch of you kids are going to be in it."

"You should get there extra early, so you can sit in the front row," I tell him. "That way, you can see me wave to you!"

Mr. Jim laughs. "Maybe I will, little lady," he says. "Maybe I will."

I add, "You won't be able to hear Lucy if you sit too far back, but don't tell her, or you might hurt her feelings."

He nods again. "Well, see you then," I tell him. Then I head back to pick out a spot to sit.

Some kids think Mr. Jim is mean. I think he's just fine!

When bedtime comes that night, I roll one way and then the other. Sleep just won't come to me. I try not to think of anything at all, but it's too hard. Imagining sheep, I start counting. Sheep one, with black spots. Sheep two, all white. Sheep three, all black. Sheep four . . .

It takes a long time to count sheep, and I do not even feel one little bit sleepy yet. Sheep don't help you sleep!

Momma checks in on me and sees that I'm still awake. "Are you havin' trouble sleeping, sugar?" she asks.

I nod. "My brain won't turn off!" I tell her.

Momma smiles. "I'll be right back," she promises.

When she comes back in a few minutes, she has my favorite mug, the one with the big pink heart on it. It's full of warm, sweet milk. "Warm milk always helps me sleep when I'm having trouble," she tells me. "Drink it all up. You'll see."

I drink the milk. At first I think it was just a dumb idea like counting the sheep. But then suddenly my eyes feel heavy, and my pink princess bed is so soft.

"Good night, sweetheart," Momma whispers. Then I slip into sleep.

In the morning, I feel great. I get dressed quickly. Then I run downstairs for breakfast. Momma has some super-special pancakes ready for me. They are heart-shaped and have raspberries in them!

Momma says, "Good morning, Queen of Hearts! Today is your big day. You better eat a good breakfast, so you can keep your energy up. We can't have our Queen too tired to say her lines tonight. Right?"

"That's right, Momma," I say.

T.J. comes in. "Guess what, Kylie Jean?" he says.

"What?" I ask.

"Daddy's gonna drive us to school today, since it's your special day," my brother says.

I clap my hands. "Yay!" I say. "That's way better than taking the bus!"

"Yeah," T.J. says. "Mean ol' Mr. Jim won't make your day start off good."

I frown. "Mr. Jim isn't mean," I tell him. "I really like him. He's going to come see my play!"

T.J. looks surprised. "Really?" he asks.

"Yeah," I say. "So don't you go bein' mean about my friend Mr. Jim!"

Chapter Thirteen
In the Spotlight

When I get to school, Lucy and Cara are
waiting for me.

"Can you believe it?" Lucy says. "Today is the
day! We're doing the play!"

We squeal and hug each other. Then Ms.
Corazón says, "Okay, everybody, let's get moving!"

It is crazy in the auditorium. Everyone is
rushing around and talking all at once. One girl
cries because her makeup makes her look funny.
One boy's costume is missing. Finally, we are all
dressed and ready.

"Ten minutes till showtime!" Ms. Corazón announces. "Everyone needs to get backstage to wait!"

All of the Alices wait together. I am wearing the dress and wig, because I go first. It is getting very noisy in the theater. Everybody in the whole school is coming in and finding a place to sit.

I peek through the curtain and see about a million kids and parents waiting to see us. Momma, Daddy, Pa, Nanny, Granny, and Pappy are all there to see us.

Cara looks out too. "Wow!" she whispers. "We're going to be famous!"

Mr. Peterson walks onstage. "Ladies and gentlemen, you are in for a treat," he says. "Ms. Corazón's class will now perform *Alice in Wonderland.*"

Everyone claps, and I step onto the stage. For just a second, I can't remember my lines. The bright stage lights are blinding me. There are so many people. I open my mouth, and nothing comes out.

Everyone is silent.

Then suddenly I remember what to do. It's just like I'm saying my lines with Ugly Brother, but instead I'm talking to kids in my class. I don't miss a single line.

As soon as I'm done, I rush to change into my Queen costume. Ms. Corazón helps me.

"You look great," she tells me. "You'll do a very good job!"

Then I have to wait backstage until it is time for the Queen of Hearts to go out. I don't worry at all this time. I shout, extra loud, "Off with their heads!" Then I wave at Mr. Jim, sitting in the front row.

Before I know it, Lucy is pretending to wake up and stretch. She says, "I had a very strange dream." Then the lights go off, and the curtain closes.

All of the kids return to the stage. The curtain goes up and lights come on. We take a bow. The room is loud with everyone clapping.

I hear someone shouting, "Bravo!"

Daddy comes to the stage. "Kylie Jean, you will always be my little queen," he says. Then he hands me a bunch of red roses and a little heart-shaped box of candy.

"Thank you, Daddy!" I say. I smell my roses. "These are the prettiest flowers in the whole wide world, and I love you to the moon and back."

I give him a big squeezy hug. People are still clapping, so I run back to the center of the stage and take another bow. My heart is pounding from excitement. I feel like a star!

Chapter Fourteen
More Spots

When I get home from school, Ugly Brother comes right over to me to congratulate me. He licks me on the face.

"You're licking the Queen!" I tell him, laughing.

He barks, "Ruff, ruff."

I head to the bathroom to wash off my special stage makeup. When I look in the mirror, I see a red polka dot on my cheek.

I shout, "Momma, come quick! I have the Chicken Spots now!"

Momma dashes in and takes a good long look at my face. Then she pulls my shirt up to look at my tummy. It's covered with spots. One of them looks like a little red heart.

Momma sighs. "You must have gotten them at school," she says.

"I borrowed Paula's costume," I whisper. "But I didn't touch her! Not even when I gave her a cookie!"

"You will be the Queen of Chicken Pox for the next two weeks," Momma says. "You'll have to stay in bed and drink lots of juice."

"Okay," I say. I don't care. Being sick will give me lots of time to make a plan. Being the Queen of Hearts was really fun, but my real dream is to be a beauty queen!

Marci Bales Peschke was born in Indiana, grew up in Florida, and now lives in Texas with her husband, two children, and a feisty black-and-white cat named Phoebe. She loves reading and watching movies.

When **Tuesday Mourning** was a little girl, she knew she wanted to be an artist when she grew up. Now, she is an illustrator who lives in South Pasadena, CA. She especially loves illustrating books for kids and teenagers. When she isn't illustrating, Tuesday loves spending time with her husband, who is an actor, and their two sons.

Glossary

character (KA-rik-tur)—one of the people in a play

costume (KOSS-toom)—clothes worn by actors or people dressing in disguise

memorize (MEM-uh-rize)—to learn something by heart

part (PART)—a character or role in a play or film

performance (pur-FOR-muhnss)—the public presentation of a play, movie, or piece of music

rehearsal (ri-HURSS-uhl)—practice for a performance

role (ROHL)—the part that a person acts in a play

set (SEHT)—the stage or scenery for a play

stagehand (STAYJ-hand)—a person who helps backstage during the performance of a play

tryout (TRYE-out)—a trial or test to see if a person is qualified to do something, such as perform a role in a play

understudy (UHN-dur-stuh-dee)—a person who can step in to play a role if another actor is sick or cannot perform

Talk!

1. Why was Paula mean to Kylie Jean and her friends?

2. Would you rather have a big part in a play or a small part? Why? Explain your answer.

3. What do you think happens after this story ends?

Be Creative!

1. Kylie Jean's goal is to be a beauty queen. What's your number-one dream? Write about it.

2. Who is your favorite character in this story? Draw a picture of that person. Then write a list of five things you know about them.

3. Design a poster advertising the performance of *Alice and Wonderland*. Don't forget to include the names of the stars!

I just loved being the Queen of Hearts! You can make your own special heart-shaped sandwiches. Just make sure to ask a grown-up for permission!

Love, Kylie Jean

From Momma's Kitchen

THE QUEEN'S SANDWICH
Makes: 1 sandwich

YOU NEED:
1 four-inch heart-shaped cookie cutter

2 slices of your favorite bread

Your favorite sandwich fillings (peanut butter and jelly, or cheese, or tuna salad, or turkey and lettuce, or whatever you like best!)

1. Put your favorite fillings onto one slice of the bread. (My favorite is strawberry jelly on whole-wheat bread!)

2. Put the other piece of bread on top.

3. Use the cookie cutter to cut a heart shape out of the middle of the sandwich. (You can throw away the outsides, but I like to eat mine!)

4. Serve and enjoy! Yum-o!

Kylie Jean

has one BIG dream . . .
to be a beauty queen!

Available from Picture Window Books
www.capstonepub.com

THE FUN DOESN'T STOP HERE!

Discover more at www.capstonekids.com

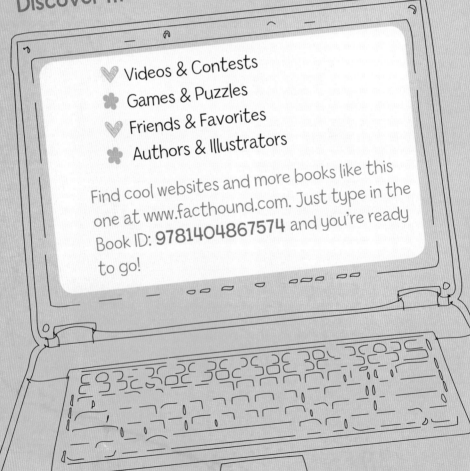

- 💜 Videos & Contests
- ❀ Games & Puzzles
- 💜 Friends & Favorites
- ❀ Authors & Illustrators

Find cool websites and more books like this one at www.facthound.com. Just type in the Book ID: **9781404867574** and you're ready to go!